The Tale of
Bambu Mouse

For Jasper,
enjoy the
Bambu
adventure!
Xie Xie
Marianne
Bouldin

Marianne Bouldin

with illustrations by Sarah Kaufman

Bambu Mouse Press

Published by Bambu Mouse Press
4000 Cathedral Avenue Northwest, No. 703B
Washington, DC 20016
www.bambumouse.com

Distributed by Bambu Mouse Press

For ordering information or special discounts for bulk purchases, please contact orders@bambumouse.com

Text design and composition by Greenleaf Book Group LLC
Cover design Sarah Kaufman and Greenleaf Book Group LLC
Illustrations by Sarah Kaufman

Publisher's Cataloging-In-Publication Data
(Prepared by The Donohue Group, Inc.)
Bouldin, Marianne.
    The tale of Bambu Mouse / by Marianne Bouldin ; illustrated by Sarah Kaufman.—1st ed.
      p. : ill. ; cm.
    Summary: A wicked storm sweeps Bambu Mouse away from her home in the forest of sky-high bamboo trees in a remote corner of China to the large city of Shanghai and beyond. The curious young mouse wanders through picturesque landscapes where she meets new friends.
    Interest age level: 000–006.
    ISBN: 978-1-4507-1236-1
    1. Mice—China—Juvenile fiction. 2. Curiosity—Juvenile fiction. 3. Friendship—Juvenile fiction.
4. China—Description and travel—Juvenile fiction. 5. Mice—China—Fiction. 6. Curiosity—Fiction.
7. Friendship—Fiction. 8. China—Description and travel—Fiction. I. Kaufman, Sarah (Sarah Elizabeth), 1973- II. Title. III. Title: Bambu Mouse
PZ7.B68 Ta 2010

Part of the Tree Neutral™ program, which offsets the number of trees consumed in the production and printing of this book by taking proactive steps, such as planting trees in direct proportion to the number of trees used: www.treeneutral.com

TreeNeutral

Manufactured by Imago on acid-free paper
Manufactured in Guangdong, China in August 2010
GLJ0063

10 11 12 13 14 15   10 9 8 7 6 5 4 3 2 1
First Edition

For Luke and Riley

Sincere thanks to:

Amy, Annie, Bill & Bob, Gary, Jane, Jen & Jingli,
Kathy, Ken, Lynne, Meg, Peanut, Peggy, Riffi, Steve & Wei

My name is Bambu Mouse and I am an only child. I live in a forest of sky-high bamboo trees. Here I am with Mama and Baba.
maa-maa   baa-baa

One day a great storm came. The creaking sound of the trees grew loud and a grumbling rose up from the ground. The lightning slashed the night sky and thunder roared as deep as a lion's cry.

It rained and rained and the fierce wind howled. The branches that Mama and Baba had neatly stacked away scattered far and wide on the forest floor.

I ate the bamboo leaves until I became very drowsy. Mama made my bed in the soft tall grasses and I fell into a deep sleep.

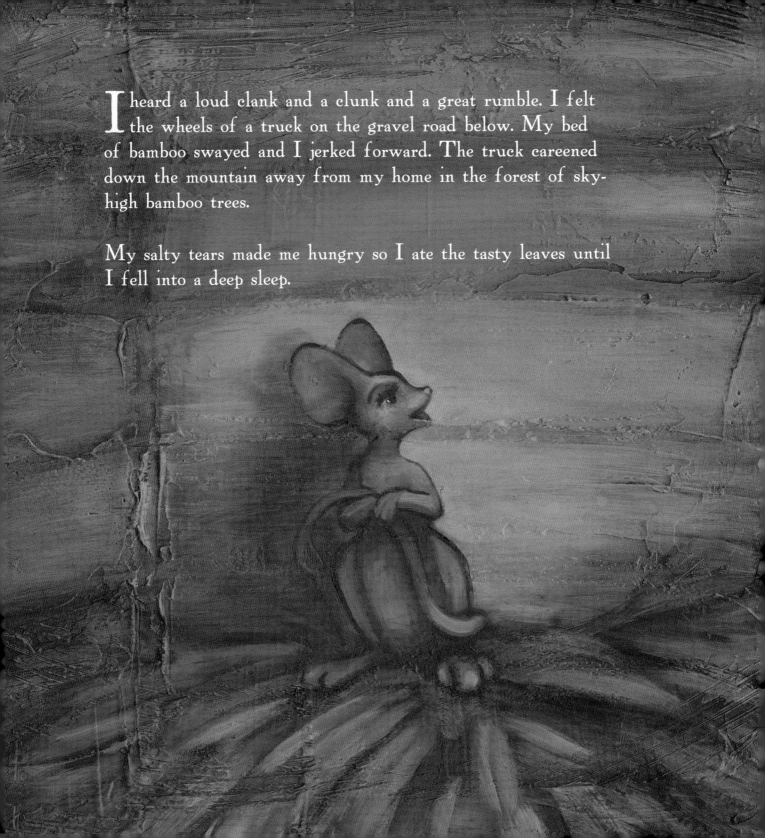

I heard a loud clank and a clunk and a great rumble. I felt the wheels of a truck on the gravel road below. My bed of bamboo swayed and I jerked forward. The truck careened down the mountain away from my home in the forest of sky-high bamboo trees.

My salty tears made me hungry so I ate the tasty leaves until I fell into a deep sleep.

When I awoke, I climbed to the top of the pile of bamboo trees. A forest of tall buildings filled the bright blue sky. The bamboo branches and I had been carried away from Mama and Baba on a flatbed truck.

I climbed down to the side of the road. I was all alone.

nee-how

Suddenly, a voice said, "Ni hao, Bambu Mouse. I am
Lao Wu Gui, Old Wise Turtle. Your tail is very handsome."

laow-woo-gway

"Xie-xie. Thank you, Lao Wu Gui. Where am I?"

shee-yay shee-yay

"We are on the banks of the lake in the middle of the city of Shanghai. See the ancient teahouse? Climb on my back and I will take you there."

"What is the name of the flower floating on the lake?"

"That is a lotus—a magical plant that grows up from roots deep in the water."

"Can you swim a little closer? It smells so sweet and I think I see . . ."

Lao Wu Gui swam closer to the lotus. I stretched my body long and I wiggled my nose to smell the flower's scent. As I gazed into the flower, I was certain I saw Mama and Baba.

"Look!"

But a gust of wind swept us away from the lotus flower in the middle of the lake in the city of Shanghai.

"Please go back, Lao Wu Gui. I saw Mama and Baba in the magical lotus."

"The lotus shows what is in your heart, Bambu Mouse," Lao Wu Gui said softly.

"Home is always in the center of your heart, exactly where it belongs."

I slid down Lao Wu Gui's back into the grass.

"Xie-xie. Thank you. I will always remember you."

And when I said the words, my heart opened and my mind's eye took an everlasting photo of Lao Wu Gui, Old Wise Turtle.

I was alone on the banks of the lake in the middle of the city of Shanghai. The forest of buildings sparkled with twinkling lights.

I thought of Mama and Baba and I felt sad.

But then I remembered that home was in my heart and would always be with me.

I fell into a deep sleep.

"Chee-Chee, Chee-Chee!"

I awoke with a start. What was that strange sound?
A bright green bug jumped through the air out of
the night sky and landed directly in front of me.

She shouted, "Who are you? Who are you?"

"Ni hao. I am Bambu Mouse. Who are you?"

shee-shoo-eye

"I am Xishuai, Joyful Cricket. Did you hear me?"

"Of course I heard you. What do you want?"

"I want to show you the full moon and the children and the lanterns in the parade."

"Oh, did I say the full moon?"

I rubbed the sleep from my eyes and considered the situation. This green bug was cheerful and I did feel a little lonely.

"Why not? Let's go, Xishuai."

you-bing

"Oh, Bambu Mouse. Eat a Yue bing, a moon cake, it is filled with yummy red bean paste. It is as round as the full moon. See it setting behind the forest of tall buildings?"

Before I could point to Mama and Baba in the full moon . . .

Xishuai shouted, "Now I must go!"

"Xie-xie. Thank you. I will always remember you."

And when I said the words, my heart opened and my mind's eye took an everlasting photo of Xishuai, Joyful Cricket.

The moon disappeared behind the forest of buildings. I inched closer to the parade of children dancing to the festival music.

A boy with blue pajamas stooped to take a small stone from his slipper.

I saw my chance and leaped onto his red lantern.

We marched along in the parade. Without any warning whatsoever, the boy with the blue pajamas stopped and I toppled forward.

I grabbed the pole with my tiny toes and slid all the way down the slippery surface until I landed on the boy's shoulder.

"Oops."

The boy with the blue pajamas turned and greeted me, "Ni hao, Bambu Mouse. My name is Ge-ge, Older Brother."

guh-guh

Ge-ge took me to the house where he lived with his Mama. He lifted me from his shoulder and gently carried me to rest on a blue blanket that matched his pajamas. I closed my eyes and fell into a deep sleep.

In the morning, I greeted Ge-ge. "Ni hao, Ge-ge. How did you know who I was? You looked like you were expecting me, yet I never introduced myself. I am Bambu Mouse."

hen-rong-yee
"Hen rongyi—that is easy to explain. I dreamed that I would have a Xiao mei-mei, a little sister."
shee-aow may-may

"But I am a mouse and you are a boy. We are so different, we cannot be related."

"Why not? What does it matter that we are different? It is only important that we love each other just as we are."

"I always wished for a brother," I told Ge-ge, "and what you say is true—that as long as we love each other . . ."

"Yes!" Ge-ge interrupted me. "We are both only children. Now we will have each other. I will take you everywhere; to school, to the park, and when you get tired I will carry you in this cricket cage."

boo-sheen
"Bu xing! No way! You cannot put me in a cage."

"I am sorry you must go," Ge-ge said.

"Xie- xie. Thank you. I will always remember you."

And when I said the words, my heart opened and my mind's eye took an everlasting photo of Ge-ge, Older Brother.

I left the warmth of the blue silk blanket. Even though I was not sure where my adventure would take me, I knew I was no longer alone.

I repeated what Ge-ge had said, "all that matters is that we love each other," over and over again.

I hopped from stone to stone along a pretty path on the banks of the lake in the city of Shanghai until I saw a brown rabbit sitting at the base of a peach tree.

"Ni hao. Why are you sitting here?"

The rabbit opened her blue eyes and looked at me. "Do you even need to ask? Sit next to me. We can breathe in the sweet smells together.

too-tzuh

"I am Tuzi, Patient Rabbit. And you must be Bambu Mouse. I've heard about you."

It didn't take long for me to grow impatient.

The sweet smells from the peach tree made me
very hungry. I watched Tuzi sit gracefully with
her legs crossed and her arms folded.

"How long are we going to sit here?" I asked.

on-jing
"Anjing. Be quiet. We sit until the peach ripens
in the tree. When it is ready, it will fall."

I closed my eyes and my breath slowed. I sniffed
in the warm scent of peach, and there I saw
Mama and Baba smiling at me.

Kerplunk! A peach dropped to the ground. Tuzi
opened her eyes and grinned. "Let's eat!"

W e bit into the peach and Tuzi said, "Patience is important. It takes time for fruit to ripen, but it does. You have to be still and wait. That is how you practice patience."

"Xiè-xie. Thank you. I will always remember you."

And when I said the words, my heart opened and my mind's eye took an everlasting photo of Tuzi, Patient Rabbit.

I hopped from stone to stone along the pretty path on the banks of the lake in the middle of the city of Shanghai.

I had seen Mama and Baba in the magical lotus. And I saw them in the full moon above the forest of buildings. While I had been practicing patience, Mama and Baba were at home in the forest of sky-high bamboo trees. I missed Mama and Baba.

In my heart and through my mind's eye, I saw the everlasting photos of my new friends:

Lao Wu Gui, Old Wise Turtle, gave me the courage to know that home is always within my heart exactly where it belongs.

Xishuai, Joyful Cricket, showed me the wonder of the full moon.

Ge-ge, Older Brother, loved me just as I am.

And Tuzi, Patient Rabbit, taught me to be still.

Before I fell asleep on the mound of soft grasses on the banks of the lake in the middle of the city of Shanghai, I saw my friends watching over me. Xishuai was showing me the way.

Tomorrow the flatbed truck will come and take me to the forest of sky-high bamboo trees.

And back to Mama and Baba.

Glossary

Anjing (on-jïng) 安静 . . . . Be Quiet

Baba (baa-baa) 爸爸 . . . . Father

Bu Xing (boo-sheen) 不行 . . . . No Way

Ge-Ge (guh-guh) 哥哥 . . . . Older Brother

Hen Rongyi (hen-rong-yee) 很容易 . . . . Very Easy

Lao Wu Gui (laow-woo-gway) 老乌龟 . . . . . Old Wise Turtle

Mama (maa-maa) 妈妈 . . . . Mother

Ni Hao (nee-how) 你好 . . . . Hello

Tuzi (too-tzuh) 兔子 . . . . Rabbit

Xiao Mei-Mei (shee-aow may-may) 小妹妹 . . . . Little Sister

Xie-Xie (shee-yay shee-yay) 谢谢 . . . . Thank You

Xishuai (shee-shoo-eye) 蟋蟀 . . . . Cricket

Yue Bing (you-bing) 月饼 . . . . Moon Cake